1/98-3

Books by Sigmund Brouwer

Lightning on Ice Series
#1 *Rebel Glory*
#2 *All-Star Pride*
#3 *Thunderbird Spirit*
#4 *Winter Hawk Star*
#5 *Blazer Drive*
#6 *Chief Honor*

Short Cuts Series
#1 *Snowboarding to the Extreme . . . Rippin'*
#2 *Mountain Biking to the Extreme . . . Cliff Dive*
#3 *Skydiving to the Extreme . . . 'Chute Roll*
#4 *Scuba Diving to the Extreme . . . Off the Wall*

CyberQuest Series
#1 *Pharaoh's Tomb*
#2 *Knight's Honor*
#3 *Pirate's Cross*
#4 *Outlaw's Gold*
#5 *Soldier's Aim*
#6 *Galilee Man*

The Accidental Detectives Mystery Series

Winds of Light Medieval Adventures

Adult Books
Double Helix
Blood Ties

QUEST 5
SOLDIER'S AIM

SIGMUND BROUWER

Thomas Nelson, Inc.
Nashville

To Martyn Godfrey,
who writes great stuff!

Soldier's Aim
Quest 5 in the *CyberQuest* Series

Copyright © 1997
by Sigmund Brouwer

Published in Nashville, Tennessee,
by Tommy Nelson™, a division of Thomas Nelson, Inc.

Managing Editor: Laura Minchew
Project Editor: Beverly Phillips
Cover illustration: Kevin Burke

Library of Congress Cataloging-in-Publication Data

Brouwer, Sigmund, 1959–
    Soldier's aim / Sigmund Brouwer.
        p. cm. — (CyberQuest ; 5)
    Summary: As the test of his faith in virtual reality continues,
Mok, a welfaro from the slums of twenty-first century Old
Newyork, finds himself helping endangered Jews in Nazi-
occupied Paris in 1943.
    ISBN 0-8499-4038-9
    [1. Virtual reality—Fiction.   2. Holocaust, Jewish (1939–
1945)—Fiction.   3. World War, 1939–1945—Fiction   4. Science
Fiction   5. Christian life—Fiction.]   I. Title.   II. Series:
Brouwer, Sigmund, 1959–   CyberQuest ; 5.
PZ7.B79984So   1997
[Fic]—dc21   97-27850
                                                       CIP
                                                        AC

Printed in the United States of America
97 98 99 00 01 02 OPM 9 8 7 6 5 4 3 2 1

146-9

CYBERQUEST SERIES TERMS

BODYWRAP — a sheet of cloth that serves as clothing.

THE COMMITTEE — a group of people dedicated to making the world a better place.

MAINSIDE — any part of North America other than Old Newyork.

MINI-VIDCAM — a hidden video camera.

NETPHONE — a public telephone with a computer keypad. For a minimum charge, users can send e-mail through the Internet.

OLD NEWYORK — the bombed out island of Manhattan transformed into a colony for convicts and the poorest of the poor.

TECHNOCRAT — an upper class person who can read, operate computers, and make much more money than a Welfaro.

'TRIC SHOOTER — an electric gun that fires enough voltage to stun its target.

VIDTRANS — a video transmitter.

VIDWATCH — a watch with a mini television screen.

WATERMAN — a person who sells pure water.

WELFARO — a person living in the slums in Old Newyork.

THE GREAT WATER WARS—A.D. 2031. *In the year* A.D. *2031 came the great Water Wars. The world's population had tripled during the previous thirty years. Worldwide demand for fresh, unpolluted water grew so strong that countries fought for control of water supplies. The war was longer and worse than any of the previous world wars. When it ended, there was a new world government, called the World United. The government was set up to distribute water among the world countries and to prevent any future wars. But it took its control too far.*

World United began to see itself as all important. After all, it had complete control of the world's limited water supplies. It began to make choices about who was "worthy" to receive water.

Very few people dared to object when World United denied water to criminals, the poor, and others it saw as undesirable. People were afraid of losing their own water if they spoke up.

One group, however, saw that the government's actions were wrong. These people dared to speak—Christians. They knew that only God should have control of their lives. They knew that they needed to stand up to the government for those who could not. Because of this, the government began to persecute the Christians and outlawed the Christian church. Some people gave up their beliefs to continue to receive an allotment of government water. Others refused and either joined underground churches or became hunted rebels, getting their water on the black market.

In North America, only one place was safe for the rebel Christians. The island of Old Newyork. The bombings of the great Water Wars had destroyed much of it, and the government used the entire island as a prison. The government did not care who else fled to the slums of those ancient street canyons.

Old Newyork grew in population. While most newcomers were criminals, some were these rebel Christians. Desperate for freedom, they entered this lion's den of lawlessness.

Limited water and supplies were sent from Mainside to Old Newyork, but some on Mainside said that any was too much to waste on the slums. When the issue came up at a World Senate meeting in 2049, it was decided that Old Newyork must be treated like a small country. It would have to provide something to the world in return for water and food.

When this new law went into effect, two things happened in the economy of this giant slum. First, work gangs began stripping steel from the skyscrapers. Anti-pollution laws on Mainside made it expensive to manufacture new steel. Old steel, then, was traded for food and water.

Second, when a certain Mainside business genius got caught evading taxes in 2053, he was sent to Old Newyork. There he quickly saw a new business opportunity—slave labor.

Old Newyork was run by criminals and had no laws. Who was there to stop him from forcing people to work for him?

Within a couple of years, the giant slum was filled with bosses who made men, women, and children work at almost no pay. They produced clothing on giant sewing machines and assembled cheap computer products. Even boys and girls as young as ten years old worked up to twelve hours a day.

Christians in Old Newyork, of course, fought against this. But it was a battle the Christians lost over the years. Criminals and factory bosses used ruthless violence to control the slums.

Christianity was forced to become an underground movement in the slums. Education, too, disappeared. As did any medical care.

Into this world, Mok was born.

PROLOGUE

OLD NEWYORK—A.D. 2076. With imagination, it was possible to see that a large tunnel had once curved through the ruins where Benjamin Rufus and the woman stood.

Shafts of sunlight shining through cracks in the street above gave an almost eerie view of the remains. Dozens of broken slabs of concrete—some three times the height of a man, some worn and crumbled to less than a foot tall—had fallen against each other, leaving large and small jumbled openings in all directions.

"Subway," Benjamin Rufus whispered. "This was once the subway."

His overcoat hung on him, showing him to be thin and stooped. His gray hair was cropped short above a tired face. He coughed deeply after he spoke, so she had to wait to ask her question.

"Subway?"

"Before the Water Wars," he said, "trains . . ."

He stopped, seeing in her eyes that she did not understand *train*.

". . . large steel boxes on wheels that moved people ran through here. The bombs of the war must have collapsed the tunnels."

Her smile was timid. "You know much."

He returned her smile, looking past the dirt smudged like shoe polish on her face. She was only shoulder high to him, dressed in rags, with a shawl covering most of her head.

"You were born here," he said. "I was not."

She looked at the ground, pausing to gather the courage to speak, then lifted her head again.

"Zubluk," she whispered, "the most feared ganglord of all. He said he knew you. How can that be if you were not born here?"

The old man closed his eyes, recalling his past. "It is a long story," he answered. "*If* we have time, I will tell you."

"We have time," she said. "I know Zubluk will not rest until he finds you. But here you will be safe. Not once have the work gangs found me here."

She shuddered at the memories of the giant brutish ganglord and his bodyguards. "But if you go above ground . . ."

Only an hour earlier, they had escaped Zubluk. They had been above, where the abandoned, steel-scavenged skyscrapers formed the street canyons that towered over the slum's shacks.

Benjamin Rufus nodded and began coughing again. This longer, harder fit shook his body.

She left him quickly, disappearing behind a giant slab. She returned with a blanket, which she wrapped around his shoulders.

"Thank you," he said. "You have offered me safety and warmth, but I do not even know your name."

"Terza," she replied simply.

"My name is Benjamin Rufus," he said formally. Nothing about him gave her a clue that until taking a ferry across the Hudson River into Old Newyork the night before, he had been one of the wealthiest and most powerful men on Mainside. Now his name was as useless to him as the fortune and freedom he had left behind. The World United government did not permit anyone to cross the rivers back to Mainside. Taking a ferry into Old Newyork was a one-way trip; the Mainside shores were guarded by land mines and soldiers with dogs.

"You took a risk to save me," he said. "Yet you know nothing about me. Why put your life in danger?"

"I listened to your words to the crowd," replied Terza. "That was enough. You spoke to my heart. It is as empty as you said. To hear that my body was more than flesh, that I had something more . . . a soul . . . it was like clear, cold water to a dry throat. I want to know more about God. About his Son. It seemed worth the risk to find the hope you described."

"God builds an emptiness into each one of us," he said. "It remains empty until we find him. Nothing else will fill it. Not money, not fame, not excitement. Believing that God came to earth as Christ, and seeking God through the Son will fill that emptiness. It brings life beyond death."

"How do you know this?" Terza asked. "I have never heard of such things . . ."

Benjamin Rufus sat down, using one of the

concrete slabs as a bench. "Are there no Christians in Old Newyork?"

She frowned. "I don't think so. Unless you mean Churchians. But what little I know of them sounds nothing like the message you bring."

The frown he returned was question enough.

"They hold secret meetings," she answered. "They have rules. Many rules. Those who don't follow the rules are condemned. They remain friends with only each other and do not accept those who do not share their beliefs."

Rufus shook his head in sadness. "Like the Pharisees of Christ's time."

He saw the question in her eyes.

"I'm sorry to say I have an advantage." Benjamin Rufus sighed. "Here in Old Newyork two or three generations have lived without education. No one can read. There are more workers than work. No medicine, no technology. The slave system forces children to work in factories. You can't be blamed for what you do not know. Just as I cannot take pride in what my background has given me."

"I know you come from Mainside," she said, "even though you have not told me so. You could not be here because the government sent you as a prisoner, otherwise your forehead would be marked. Why are you here?"

"The answer is simple," he said after a moment's reflection. "There have been two or three generations here without an understanding of the message of Christ. They live without hope. The next generation must not live that way."

"You will pay with your life to deliver your message."

"Yes," he said. "Of that I have no doubt. I only pray it is later than sooner; where the ground is rocky and dry, many seeds must be sown in many places for the tree to grow."

The woman sat beside him. "Begin with me. Perhaps I can help put seeds in places you cannot go."

CHAPTER 1

MAINSIDE—TWENTY YEARS LATER (A.D. 2096). Cambridge sat alone in his office on the tenth floor of the luxury highrise. The only thing luxurious about the office, however, was the vastness of its view. If Cambridge raised his head from the computer screen before him, he would see sky and river and the far shoreline that marked the island of Old Newyork. Despite the money and resources available to him, he had not treated himself to expensive carpet or walnut paneling or a large desk or rare art.

In fact, his office simply held the desk at which he sat and the computer, which held his total attention. The screen showed a three-dimensional image of a young man dressed in black walking a cobblestone street on a winter afternoon.

This young man actually lay motionless on a padded cot in a smaller room just down the hallway. He was a Welfaro from the slums of Old Newyork named Mok. Tubes connected his body to a life-support machine. Other lines were taped to his shaved head and ran to a nitrogen-cooled computer. Two nurses tended his still body. Both watched his heart rate and other vital signs with

1

great care. They had instructions to call a team of medtechs and comtechs at the slightest sign of trouble.

Despite the short physical distance between them, Cambridge and Mok shared the same space. Cyberspace. Mok lived it as Cambridge watched.

Cambridge rested his chin on his hand. The thoughts crossing his mind added intensity to his almost hawklike face.

Please God, do not let Mok fail, Cambridge prayed. *He's come this far. Don't let him fail.* Mok's success was crucial to swing the one or two important Senate votes needed to keep heat bombs from destroying Old Newyork.

Yet, watching the computer screen, Cambridge could not hide from the knowledge of how thin the line was between success and failure. The cyberprogram linked Mok's mind to a virtual reality so close to life that if Mok died in cyberspace, it would scramble the nerve circuits in his brain, killing him in real time as well.

Worse, this would be Mok's most difficult cybertest. And he had come so close to the end . . .

Cambridge thought with pride of the other stages of Mok's cyberadventure. Egypt, the test of justice. The Holy Land castle siege that tested his beliefs. A pirate ship that helped him learn to share those beliefs. The Wild West, where he was tempted with riches over truth. And now . . .

And now—Cambridge slammed his hand down on his desk in anger—Mok must face betrayal. Not

2

betrayal built into the events of virtual reality, where every choice Mok made could shift the program in almost infinite directions.

No. This betrayal came from one of the twelve Committee members. Betrayal after nearly two decades of working together in secrecy to follow the plans laid by Benjamin Rufus.

So, instead of observing Mok with the growing hope of success, Cambridge was forced to watch the computer screen for a cyberassassin.

Even now, Cambridge could hardly believe it.

One of the Committee had sent a killer into cyberspace. That killer's only goal was to stop Mok at any cost.

CHAPTER 2

CYBERSPACE—PARIS (A.D. 1943). Gray sky. Clouds hung low over drab, dirty buildings. Traces of snow drifted onto the cobblestone streets. Several parked vehicles half blocked the sidewalk. Men and women, with heads bowed, walked the sidewalks in heavy, dark overcoats, their breath becoming small clouds of vapor in the late afternoon winter chill.

Mok noticed all of this, but only briefly.

His attention focused on what was far ahead of him, where the cobblestone street disappeared between the cramped buildings that lined both sides. At the top of the hill, he saw five men marching toward him. They wore uniforms and each carried a rifle slung over his left shoulder. As the men marched down the slope of the hill, Mok saw the helmets of another row of soldiers begin to top the hill from the other side. The helmets rose higher followed by shoulders, then waists, until those soldiers, too, crested the hill and began to march down toward Mok.

Followed by another five.

And another five.

Row after row of soldiers filled the street. And behind all of this, Mok heard a rumble, growing louder each passing second.

Yet the men and women on the sidewalks continued their business as if nothing were strange about waves of soldiers filling the street.

As for Mok, the rumbling noise gave him an eerie dread. It was a sound so unnatural, so ominous, that without realizing his feet were moving, he found himself in an alley.

It cut his view of the street to the small gap just ahead of him, but it seemed the safest move, considering he had no idea where he was or what was happening.

Seconds later, the first row of soldiers passed by the alley, marching precisely in step.

Earlier, Mok might have thought this was a twisted dream caused by polluted drinking water. In the slums of Old Newyork, glo-glo water was all too common.

But Mok had long given up the idea that he was trapped in a dream. Too much that was too strange and too real had happened. He was no longer one of countless thousands of Welfaros trying to survive in the grimy street canyons of Old Newyork. . . . not since the afternoon in the tunnels beneath the city.

Mok had faced a man with a strange weapon, one that shot an arc of blue light into Mok's chest. Mok had awakened in ancient Egypt, where sand burned his feet, and blows against him had actually drawn blood. He'd quickly learned it was no dream. Especially when events had brought him to an execution order he had barely survived.

Just as he'd begun to believe his new world was

real, darkness had spun him to an ancient castle. From there, after surviving a siege, Mok had awakened on a pirate ship, facing a hurricane and savage raids. On that ship, there'd been a monster of a man who'd attempted to murder Mok. As the brute had slashed a knife toward Mok's chest, he'd been thrown into darkness again, only to wake up in grassland prairies. A Pawnee Indian had taken him to a camp, where he'd learned to handle a six-shooter and learned to judge a man's actions, not his words. And now . . .

Here. Wherever this was. With Old Newyork long behind him, Mok had learned that he could do little in each new situation beyond wait and watch.

The soldiers continued to pass by him. And the rumbling continued to grow.

An old man staggered into the alley, bent almost double by the weight of a sack on his back. The man lurched toward Mok, intent on passing through the alley.

Mok saw the old man's face only briefly. Deep wrinkles sketched a picture of sorrow, pain, and weariness. It pierced Mok's heart to instinctive compassion.

The rumbling was so loud that Mok did not try to speak. Instead, he touched the old man's shoulder as the man passed by.

The old man dropped the sack and half lifted his arms, as if trying to ward off a blow. Mok saw his clothes were ragged and that the man had a large six-pointed yellow star sewn on one sleeve.

"No!" Mok shouted over the rumbling noise. He pointed at the fallen sack. Potatoes had spilled onto the cobblestones. "Let me help carry!"

Before the old man could reply, two things happened.

The first was something Mok did not understand until it was explained to him later. Nothing in Old Newyork had taught him about the machines of war. Following the soldiers, German Panzer tanks passed the alley. Their loud engines drove steel treads that crunched and roared over the rough cobblestones. From the corner of his eye, Mok saw the long barrels and the turrets, the dull green plating of the tank shell, and the series of wheels that turned the caterpillar treads.

The second thing, however, Mok did understand; he had seen the gangs in Old Newyork.

A dozen kids swarmed the alley.

They began to pelt the old man with sticks and stones and garbage.

CHAPTER 3

INSTANT ANGER SWEPT through Mok. He dashed forward.

Although Mok was outnumbered, the boys were younger and smaller. And the boys were not filled with rage. Mok snatched a stick from one of them and began to swing.

They backed off in surprise. Something in Mok's face turned their surprise to fear. Wordlessly, like a pack of wolves working together, the boys spun on their heels and dashed back toward the street.

Mok stood with his fists clenched around the stick, his chest heaving. He watched until the last of the boys disappeared. Only then, as he calmed his breathing, did he turn back to the old man.

Mok gasped.

Blood ran down the man's face from a gash on his forehead.

Mok searched his pockets.

In different times, he'd found himself in different attire. In Egypt, there had been a white tunic. In the Holy Land castle, metal armor. On the pirate ship, little more than a collection of rags. In the Wild West, pants and a shirt of rough fabric.

Here, he wore black pants and a loose black sweater beneath his black overcoat. As always, he

9

had no idea how it happened. He had just learned to accept it.

In his pockets, Mok found a handkerchief and bits of colorful paper.

Mok let the paper fall to the cobblestones and stepped forward with the handkerchief to press it against the old man's forehead.

"Money," the man said, his eyes wide. "Don't let the wind take it!"

Mok kept his hand gentle against the man's forehead. He half turned to see where the man was pointing. All Mok saw were the bits of colored paper.

"Money?" Mok repeated. In Old Newyork, tokens of titanium were called money.

"Enough to feed my wife and me for a year!" The man struggled to get away from Mok, to reach the money.

"Paper is money?" Mok said.

"And money is food!" The man took the handkerchief from Mok. "Pick it up before those children return."

Mok did so, putting it back in his pocket. When he straightened, the man was staring oddly at him.

"I am called Mok," he said. "I hope you are not hurt badly."

"Thaddeus," the old man said. He pulled the handkerchief away and grimaced at the sight of the blood. "How have you lived your whole life without knowing money? And how do you have so much?"

Mok gave a grim smile. "I wish you could answer

those questions for me. I wish you could answer many more as well."

"You do not make sense," Thaddeus said.

Mok stooped and began to pick up the man's scattered potatoes.

"Think of me as someone newly dropped onto the street," Mok said. "And please tell me. Where are we and what year is this?"

"Paris," Thaddeus answered, more puzzled. "Nineteen hundred and forty-three."

"And that?" Mok asked, pointing at the strange thing on four wheels just beyond the alley. He'd never seen one in Old Newyork.

"An automobile. How can you not know that?"

"Automobile," Mok said, more to himself than the old man. "I *have* heard of those. From before the Water Wars."

"Water Wars?" Thaddeus echoed. "This is the Second World War. The Germans now occupy Paris. What are the Water Wars?"

Mok had gathered the remaining potatoes. Then he lifted the sack.

"I'll carry these," Mok said, "if you will lead."

A strange expression remained on the old man's face. "Surely you see the Star of David on my sleeve."

"Yes," Mok said, unsure of what the man meant.

"I'm a Jew," Thaddeus explained. "That's why the boys followed and tried to rob me. No one helps Jews in these times."

"I do," Mok said.

Thaddeus smiled for the first time.

"May God bless you," Thaddeus said.

Mok smiled and followed the man's slow pace. The alley twisted and turned several times. Above them were the windows of apartments, black and bleak in the dying sunshine. Garbage lined both sides of the alley.

Mok remained behind Thaddeus until the alley finally emptied onto another street.

Thaddeus stopped and moaned with horror.

At first Mok saw only the street, the drab buildings, and some gathered soldiers. On the ground, in front of one of the buildings, sat an old woman, surrounded by piles of clothing.

"Run away," she cried when she saw Thaddeus. "Run!"

He hurried toward her instead, his arms wide. "Miriam! Are you all right?"

The old lady tottered to her feet. Her face was crooked with grief.

"You should have saved yourself," she said. "You should have disappeared back into the alley."

"I could never leave you," Thaddeus said. "What happened?"

"Our home, Thaddeus," she said. "Tonight of all nights, they have taken our home."

CHAPTER 4

THADDEUS SEEMED TO GROW stronger and taller as he comforted his wife. She buried her face in his chest. He held her close with his right arm and soothed her by stroking her gray hair with his left hand.

"We have each other," Mok heard Thaddeus say to her quietly. "We have each other. We will always have our love. No one can ever take that away."

The old woman hugged him tighter. The sleeve of her overcoat had a yellow star sewn onto it.

Jews, thought Mok. *A yellow star to mark them. What were Jews? Why were they marked?*

Miriam stepped back from Thaddeus. She bit her lower lip to hold back her tears as they gazed on each other.

Sadness hit Mok. Not at their grief. But because their love was so strong. It made him aware of how alone he was.

"Why have they done this?" Thaddeus asked her.

"They said an army captain wants our home," Miriam said. Her voice trembled. "All our cherished keepsakes and furniture. Everything we've put together in our lifetime. His!"

Thaddeus whispered something else. Mok was close enough to hear, but not sure if he heard correctly.

"The radio," Thaddeus said. "Did they find the radio?"

Miriam whispered her reply. "Not yet. Nor the little book . . ."

Thaddeus shook his head in warning as he looked past her at the soldiers.

Two of them, large men armed with machine guns, walked toward the couple.

"Enough," one of the soldiers grunted. "Pick up your belongings and come with us."

"Come where?" Thaddeus asked. Not in desperation, but in anger. "Isn't it enough you take our home? You take our freedom now too?"

"We have orders to put you on a train to a work camp outside of France," the soldier said. "Move now or I will break your teeth."

The soldier lifted his machine gun and threatened the old man with the butt. He jabbed it toward Thaddeus's face for emphasis.

Until then, Mok had not moved. The scene had taken his attention so fully, he had forgotten the weight of the sack of potatoes on his shoulder.

Yet as the soldier forced Thaddeus to cower, Mok stepped toward the couple, not sure what he could do to protect them against an armed soldier, but unable to stop his impulse.

"Is this your grandson?" the soldier asked as he noticed Mok. "If so, where is his star? You know Jews who don't wear the star may be executed."

"He is not a Jew," Thaddeus said quickly. "I paid him to carry my load."

14

The soldier grinned at Mok, showing stained teeth. "I'll take the money then. You should know better than to help a Jew. Perhaps we'll put you on the train too."

Suddenly, the soldier's grin froze. He backed away from Mok and the couple.

He barked a few words in German at the other soldiers. They all stiffened and stood at attention.

Thaddeus looked behind him. His face showed instant concern.

"The Gestapo!" he hissed to Mok. "The worst of the Nazis. Walk away now as if you don't know us, and you might be safe."

"But you . . ."

"Forget about us!" Thaddeus said. "We'll pray the car is just passing by. If not, there is no need for you to suffer with us! Go! Now!"

Mok peeked over his shoulder.

A long, gleaming, black automobile glided down the street toward them. Its windows were dark. Small flags waved from the hood of the car.

Mok was paralyzed by indecision. How could he leave these people? But if he stayed, how could he help them against soldiers and the Gestapo, whatever the Gestapo was?

Mok hesitated too long.

The car stopped. Mok could not see through the darkened windows.

A tall man in a highly decorated uniform stepped out of the vehicle. All the soldiers instantly saluted. Thaddeus and Miriam huddled against each other.

"Jews?" the Gestapo officer asked, pointing at the building behind the soldiers. "From that apartment?"

"Yes," a soldier said. "These are the ones. To be shipped to a work camp. We were only following orders."

"Idiots! With all these possessions?"

"Standard procedure," the soldier stammered, "for all Jews. Let them take what they can carry."

"Not these," the Gestapo officer snapped. He pulled a pistol from a fine leather holster. He pointed it at Miriam's head. "Get into the car. Both of you."

"But we have our orders," the soldier said. "If we do not return with them, our commanding officer—"

"These Jews are helping others escape the country," the Gestapo officer snarled. "No punishment will be too harsh for them."

He waved his pistol at Thaddeus and Miriam. The soldiers fell back, and the old couple shuffled, frightened, toward the car.

The Gestapo officer swung the pistol and turned it on Mok.

"And you? What is your involvement with these Jews? Are you with them?"

To his shame, Mok wanted to lie. He wanted to deny he knew them, or had sympathy for them.

Yet the lie took too long to get to his lips. For a long moment, he stared back at the officer, while flakes of snow drifted down between them from the cold, gray sky.

"Your silence is answer enough," the man barked. "Get into the car!"

CHAPTER 5

AS THE DRIVER gunned the car forward, the Gestapo officer on the passenger side half turned to look at Mok, Miriam, and Thaddeus in the backseat. The officer lifted his hat from his head and smoothed his thick, dark hair with his hand. He had a movie star face, with black eyes and a thin mustache.

"So, my friends," he said to them, "where would you like me to take you?"

He dropped his hat in his lap and smiled at the surprise on the faces of his prisoners.

"You heard me correctly," he said, still smiling. "I am offering you freedom. Where would you like me to take you?"

"Freedom?" Thaddeus asked.

"Let me explain," the Gestapo officer said. "My name is Wolfgang and . . ."

He unbuttoned the top of his uniform, reached inside, and pulled out a silver chain. He dangled it so that on the end of the necklace they could see a six-pointed star within a circle.

"The Star of David," Miriam gasped. "A symbol of hope for the Jews. But you are a—"

"A Nazi? Sworn to dispose of the Jews?" he said. She nodded.

"Indeed, I am a high-ranking Gestapo officer. But also a secret sympathizer to the Jews. It is a crime how they are treated. My driver and I have taken to cruising the streets, looking to rescue those Jews we can. It is but little in the face of what has been happening. Yet at least I am doing what I can."

Except for the hum of tires over the cobblestones, there was silence as Miriam and Thaddeus looked at each other.

"Can we believe him?" Miriam whispered. "Do we dare hope?"

Thaddeus spoke to her in a low voice. "No, my love. This is a trap."

He repeated his words to Wolfgang, louder, almost defiant: "This is a trap."

Wolfgang arched his eyebrows. "A trap?"

"You told the soldier you were taking us because we were helping others to escape. You could not know that if you were simply driving by as you say."

The officer stared at them for at least a half minute. Then he laughed loud and long. "What priceless humor!" he finally said. "I thought I was telling the soldier a lie. So, you *have* helped other Jews escape?"

Thaddeus did not answer.

Wolfgang shook his head in admiration. "What a fortunate day. Of any who might deserve help from me, then, it would be the two of you. I give freedom to the freedom givers."

The driver made a turn. Although the streets were

crowded with people, they parted quickly for the car that so obviously carried the Nazi elite.

Wolfgang reached into a pocket of his uniform. He pulled out a thick wad of folded money.

"For you," he said, reaching over the seat. "It will help you. Now tell me, where do you want to go?"

Neither Miriam nor Thaddeus accepted the money.

Wolfgang sighed. With his other hand, he offered them his pistol.

"Here," he said. "Would I hand you this if I meant you harm?"

Mok spoke for the first time since entering the car. "Check it for bullets."

Thaddeus took the pistol. He clicked a button and the clip fell from the pistol's handle. It was full of bullets.

"Good," Mok said. "I'd hate to get tricked twice."

"Twice?" Thaddeus asked. "This has happened to you before?"

"Another time and place," Mok answered. "It's too long a story to bother telling."

"Are you satisfied?" Wolfgang interrupted. "We must hurry. If I don't return soon, I will have too many questions to answer."

"Satisfied," Thaddeus said. He handed Wolfgang back the pistol and, with a motion very smooth for a man so old, took the thick wad of money. "Turn the car around and take us to a small cafe near the river. Le Café Bordeaux."

"Le Café Bordeaux!" Miriam said. "Surely you can't mean to go there. After all, the—"

Thaddeus squeezed Miriam's knee to keep her silent.

"Le Café Bordeaux," Thaddeus said firmly.

"You must leave Paris," Wolfgang protested. "More and more they are rounding up the Jews. If you get caught again, I cannot guarantee I will be able to save you."

"Wolfgang," Thaddeus answered, "leaving the city is exactly what we intend to do."

"I don't understand," Wolfgang said. "A café? Where people meet for food and drink?"

"If you want us to escape, please take us there," Thaddeus answered. "I can say no more."

CHAPTER 6

MAINSIDE—A.D. 2096. In another office, some twenty miles away from Cambridge, another Committee member also faced a computer. He, like Cambridge, carefully watched the three-dimensional image of Mok's cyberjourney. Unlike Cambridge, however, this man's face seemed joyful.

He sat back in his chair with his feet propped on his desk. He was home alone and did not expect any interruptions.

His right hand rested on the vidphone. The number he had keyed in would connect him to the president of the World United, the most powerful man among the global union of civilized nations.

Any second now, the Committee member told himself, any second now he could hit "send" and connect the call.

He grinned at the computer screen. Any second now a brute of a man would appear among the people passing by the small café in wartime Paris.

The Committee member could clearly see the sign in the background: Le Café Bordeaux.

When this brute of a man appeared, he would bring Cambridge's plan to an end. This man had been sent to prison for murdering three people at their dinner table, then sitting down to finish their meal before robbing their house.

The president of the World United had freed him on one condition—that he allow himself to be hooked up to a virtual reality computer and sent into cyberspace. His task was simple. Kill Mok.

The mechanics had been easy to arrange. The killer was attached to a computer hundreds of miles from the Committee site. The Committee member had supplied the encryption code to allow him access to the Committee's private cybersite. Then the killer had traveled into cyberspace to search for Mok.

The cyberassassin had failed once. But Mok had expected that attack.

Here, on the streets of Paris, the killer would simply step out of the crowd and knife Mok in the chest. End of Mok. End of program. End of Old Newyork.

The Committee member smiled to think of the wealth waiting for him. He smiled wider as he saw the image of a large man with a fierce scowl move into the doorway of Le Café Bordeaux.

Moments later, the image of a dark limousine rolled to a stop in front of the café. The door opened. Mok stepped out, only a few feet away from death. The cyberassassin would kill Mok in cyberspace— Paris, 1943. And in real time—Mainside, 2096.

As he watched the killer knife Mok, the Committee member hit the send button on the vidphone.

The president of the World United had given him an order to call the moment that Mok died.

CYBERSPACE—PARIS. The Gestapo car pulled up in front of Le Café Bordeaux. Mok opened his door and stepped into the street, almost into the path of another car. The driver honked as the car nearly brushed him. Mok caught a glimpse of the driver's face, pale behind the windshield. But the car passed too quickly for him to apologize.

Mok walked around the car to the sidewalk. He gave support first to Miriam, then to Thaddeus, as they, too, stepped out of the car.

The moment they closed the door, the Gestapo car eased away and disappeared down the street. Wolfgang had no reason to stay; he had wished them well and said his good-byes as they neared the café.

Mok shivered as he looked around. The car's warmth had been much nicer than the cold twilight.

The café was a small building, sandwiched between larger buildings. The windows glowed from candlelight inside. Diners sat at tables near the windows. It looked like a warm, cheerful place.

Mok waited for Miriam and Thaddeus to move toward the café, eager to be warm again.

Instead, Thaddeus took Miriam by the arm and headed away from the building.

"Hurry," he said. "And you, too, young man. Come with us."

"But the café . . ." Mok said, confused.

"No," Thaddeus said sharply. "I don't trust Wolfgang. He may be simply letting us go to find out how Miriam and I smuggle other Jews to England."

"Smuggle?" Mok asked. A lot had happened in a short time, and he couldn't make sense of it all.

"The Nazis have done terrible things to us Jews," Thaddeus said. "Whole families have disappeared, sent to work camps. Miriam and I have worked with resistance fighters to help some Jews get out of the country. But we must do it secretly. The Jews must be smuggled out."

"I don't understand," Mok said.

"If we don't, Jews will die. Jews will—"

"I mean, I don't understand why it is so important for the Nazis to harm the Jews. What have you done to deserve such hatred?"

"It is simply that we are different. For some people, that is enough. The color of our skin perhaps. Or our different beliefs. It's a sad thing to judge people without first knowing their hearts . . ."

"And Wolfgang is enough of a man to stand against this?" Mok asked.

"If Wolfgang is truly for us, it won't matter where he thinks we went," Thaddeus said. He pointed at the warm glow of the café. "But if he wanted me to give him a clue as to where the smuggling begins, he is welcome to believe it is Le Café Bordeaux. The owner is a Jew hater and has made money turning

Jews over to the Nazis. It wouldn't surprise me, in fact, if *he* told the Nazis about Miriam and me."

"In other words," Mok said, now understanding why Miriam had first protested in the car, "if Wolfgang suspects the owner, he will harass him . . ."

Thaddeus grinned. "Exactly, my friend. Perhaps soldiers will even raid the café tonight. And in the meanwhile, twenty Jews depend on Miriam and me this evening."

"Twenty . . ." Mok didn't have time to finish his question. Thaddeus and Miriam had begun to walk away.

Mok hurried to catch up.

Without slowing down, Thaddeus said to Mok, "I have wondered whether you, too, are a spy for the Nazis. Yet my heart and mind tell me no. I take a different way home every day, so you could not have known I would be in the alley where we met. Nor could you have known a gang would attack me."

"A gang?" Miriam asked. She stopped her husband to put her hands on his face to search his eyes. Then she noticed the gash on his forehead. "Are you hurt?"

"No," he chuckled. "This young man fought them all. It could not have been a fight arranged to earn my confidence. So now, unlike I do for Wolfgang, I give him my trust."

He pulled her close and hugged her. "And, as the God we love knows, we desperately need to be able to trust someone."

"Yes," Miriam said simply. "Yes, we do."

Thaddeus turned to face Mok. Nearly all the day's light had disappeared. Shadows covered the old man's face. Snow lightly dusted the shoulders of his overcoat.

"Over the past week," Thaddeus said, "many Jews have come to us for help. We have found a place for them. Tonight all of us are to escape. To lose our home tonight is the worst timing possible . . ."

"You want me to help you reach the others?" Mok asked.

"No," Thaddeus said. "They are not far away. Miriam and I can get to them ourselves. We have until midnight to meet with them and the resistance fighters who have been helping us. However, I beg you to use that time to go to our home. I doubt the army captain has begun to move in yet, and there is something you must get for us."

"What is it?" Mok asked.

Thaddeus drew a deep breath. "For months, I have used a crystal radio to listen to Nazi broadcasts. When I can, I send news across the channel to England to whoever might be listening."

Mok hung his head. "I'm sorry," he said. "I don't understand what *crystal radio* is. Or *channel*. Or *England*. Where I come from . . ."

"There's nothing to be ashamed of," Thaddeus said quickly. "No one has complete knowledge. You, I'm sure, know things I do not."

Mok accepted this encouragement with a smile.

Thaddeus smiled back and said, "So let me explain some of what I know."

Thaddeus took a few hurried minutes to tell Mok about the crystal radio, and about the fifty miles of water between the countries of England and France. Thaddeus explained that it was so dangerous to be caught with the radio, that he would take it apart and hide the pieces when he wasn't using it.

When he finished, Mok nodded. "This radio is valuable. You want me to return to your home and retrieve it from the hiding places?"

"There is more," Thaddeus said. "Not just the radio. Something else. Something you must find and bring to us. We will be waiting in a barge—"

He noticed Mok's confused look and added, "a flat-bottomed boat—at the river's edge."

Mok waited.

"You see," Thaddeus said, "certain things come easy to some people. I was born with a head for numbers."

Miriam patted his shoulder. "What this wonderful old man is trying to tell you is that he is a genius. Truly a mathematical genius. Before the war, he lectured at the university. He has many books published on the subject of encryption."

Again, Mok asked for an explanation.

"Codes," Thaddeus answered. "No one can understand the messages sent without the key to the code. During war, it is how top-secret information is passed."

Thaddeus noticed that passersby were forced to walk around them. He waited until no one was near. Finally he spoke again.

"Young man," Thaddeus said, "I have cracked the code the Germans have used over the last few months. That information will be extremely valuable to those who fight the Germans and wish to end the war."

Mok asked, "What exactly am I looking for?"

"A small black book," Thaddeus said. "I would not ask you to put yourself in danger, but I cannot return to my home. Neither can Miriam."

"I will do my best," Mok said.

"You must do more," Thaddeus said. "Not only does the book contain the code I've cracked, but it also has hundreds of details on Germany's plans for a surprise invasion against England. If we can get this plan to the right people, the Germans can be stopped."

Thaddeus gripped Mok's shoulders and stared him in the eyes.

"Do you understand, my friend?" Thaddeus said, almost pleading. "This book can not only save thousands upon thousands of lives, but it can also change the course of history. And now it seems you are our only hope."

GETTING INTO THE APARTMENT had been simple. The streets were dark and the soldiers stationed near the building ignored Mok. Thaddeus had given Mok a key to the back downstairs entrance and to the apartment on the third floor.

Inside the apartment, Mok had no trouble finding the radio pieces. He had used a small candle in his search, and the radio components were exactly where Thaddeus had told him to look. He held them now in a small sack. Thaddeus had been clear with his instructions: take all of the pieces of the radio and discard them far away from the apartment. The Nazis must not realize that a former mathematics professor and encryption expert had been using a radio.

Simple as it had been so far, Mok's nerves were like thin copper strands being pulled tighter and tighter. The darkness beyond the tiny light of the candle unnerved him. The shadows of furniture seemed to become Nazis ready to pounce. And there was the silence, broken only by Mok's shallow breathing. At any second, he expected soldiers to burst through the door. And he would be trapped.

Mok forced himself to take a couple of deep

breaths before lack of oxygen and fear could make him dizzy. He reminded himself that all he had left to retrieve was the book . . .

A book that could change the history of the war.

Mok tried not to think of the book's importance. He looked for the painting of a sailboat along the far wall.

In a cabinet to the left of the painting, Thaddeus had said, *you will find a false bottom. Empty the bottom shelf. Then trigger the hinge by feeling for a button beneath the cabinet.*

He tiptoed across the hardwood floor, careful not to bump into anything.

The flicker of the candle finally showed him the painting. It led him to the cabinet.

Mok set his sack down on the floor.

He quietly opened the cabinet door. It held shelves of china plates and bowls, arranged neatly in rows. He got on his knees and set the candle down, then began pulling the china, piece by piece, from the bottom. When all the pieces were on the floor, Mok dropped even lower and groped beneath the cabinet. His fingers brushed the cabinet legs and finally touched a button near the back, exactly as Thaddeus had promised.

With a satisfying click, the button responded to the pressure of his finger.

Mok looked inside the cabinet and saw that the bottom of it had released upward on a spring hinge. He lifted the panel higher, and saw the small notebook in the space beneath.

Mok briefly closed his eyes in relief. He let out a breath, unaware that he had been holding it.

Mok reached for the notebook. And froze as a boot slapped the hardwood floor only inches behind him.

Before he could turn, the candle went out.

"Does it frighten you," a voice whispered in the darkness, "to think of the power this little book has given you?"

CHAPTER 9

FOR LONG, LONG MOMENTS, Mok waited for the blow against his head. He waited for the knife in his back. He waited for the kick in his kidneys.

Nothing happened.

His fear built until it rose to the point of cold anger. Mok decided to face the presence behind him, not take a blow crouched like a dog. Slowly, he stood. Slowly, he turned.

He strained his eyes in the dark. Finally, he saw the outline of someone before him. Someone chest high.

"Let me repeat my question," the voice whispered. "Does it frighten you to think of the book's power? The lives of thousands upon thousands are in your hands."

Now, Mok's mind shrieked. *Now!*

He dove forward, hoping surprise might overpower whatever weapon the intruder had.

He hit the intruder hard and low. They banged to the floor in a tumbling heap. Mok found the man's neck and grabbed and twisted. There had been times in Mok's life when he'd had to fight to save his life. He knew the feeling of desperation and how to turn it into a weapon.

The other fought back, gasping and choking.

Mok squeezed tighter.

Without warning, the intruder went limp.

Mok let go and backed away. He stood poised, ready to fight again at the slightest movement.

Seconds passed.

"Have you finished your obnoxious soldier games?" the man finally croaked. "Or must I play dead a little longer?"

Mok knew the voice.

"Stinko?" Mok asked. "I mean, Blake, is that you?"

"Yes," Blake answered. "Much against my will, I am here."

Blake! The dwarf who had appeared to guide Mok in other times and places!

"I've pegged you as nothing but trouble from the beginning," Blake continued, "and this only proves it. Don't think I'm happy because you actually re-membered to use my real name."

Mok took a moment to relight the candle. The flame showed that the dwarf's face still held all the grumpiness it had before.

"Well, don't think *I'm* happy at the way you chose to say hello after all this time," Mok snapped. "I ought to choke you again."

Blake groaned as he struggled to his feet.

"Go ahead," Blake said. "My pain can't get worse anyway. And it will give me an excuse not to de-liver my message."

Mok's mood instantly shifted away from irritation.

Blake knew something about the strange worlds Mok had entered.

"Message?" Mok demanded. "From whom? About what?"

"No, no, no, no, no," Blake said quickly, smugly—delighted at Mok's response. "You don't get those answers tonight."

"When?" Mok said, back to irritation. He set the candle on one of the cabinet's shelves. "You owe me. Or someone owes me. I didn't ask to be put into this."

"We don't ask to be born, either. But no one hands us all the answers. All we can do is search for them."

"That's what this is?" Mok demanded. He inched closer to the dwarf. "A search for answers? What kind of stupid—"

"A search, like life," Blake interrupted. "This is no different for you than any life. You have a training ground to learn and make decisions for what comes after. An opportunity to seek the answers about where you are going and why. After all, life is a quest, sometimes glorious, sometimes brutal, sometimes sad and painful, sometimes . . . hey!"

"I've figured some of this out, you know," Mok said in conversational tones, as if his hands were not again firmly around Blake's neck. "Someone is sending me through time. The same person who sends you after me and pulls you out again. How else could you and the girl follow me? And that cretin who tried to kill me. You don't even have to tell me how. I just want to know why. And if you don't tell me, I'll start squeezing and won't stop until my fingers meet in the middle."

"Nice try," Blake said, tapping his toes with impatience. "But I know you won't. And so do you."

"How do you know?" Mok asked, trying to force a sneer into his voice.

"Because you've come this far. Another type of person would never have made it out of Egypt. Let alone go through the other worlds as you did."

Mok sighed and gave up. He dropped his hands to his sides. "I hope you're enjoying yourself."

"There are moments," Blake said. "Like when I blew out your candle and whispered from behind. I'll bet you almost wet y—"

"Just give me the message," Mok said, weary now. "Isn't this part of it? You deliver a message and then go away, so I can suffer through something I don't understand."

It was Blake's turn to sigh. "If you insist on taking the fun out of it."

"I do."

"Then here it is," Blake said. "Power for the sake of power is close to evil. Yet all of us have power to some degree. And to do right with the power we have often demands lonely, difficult choices."

Mok understood the seriousness in Blake's voice.

"The book?" Mok asked quietly. "Is this the power you mean?"

"There is more than one way to get the code book to England," Blake said. "You will arrive at the boat

36

along the river in less than half an hour. I can promise you that. When you get there, think about what the book could mean to the world."

Without warning, without a shimmer, the dwarf disappeared.

CHAPTER 10

MAINSIDE. Cambridge faced the entire Committee in a conference room down the hall from Mok and his life-support machine.

Behind him, the large vidscreen was gray. Unactivated.

Cambridge waited until the Committee members were seated.

"You may be wondering why I called an emergency meeting this early in the morning," Cambridge said. "Especially since the hourly updates e-mailed to most of your home net-sites show the candidate surviving well as he learns to deal with racial hatred and the difficulties of leadership."

Cambridge looked them over, one at a time. Some wore the latest fashions of fitness suits. None bothered to dress in the togas that signified Technocrats. Few of them felt the need.

"But one of you," Cambridge continued, "believes something different. In fact, one of you is under the impression that Mok died last night."

Instant babble greeted Cambridge's statement.

He held up his hand for silence.

Instead of speaking again, however, Cambridge clicked a remote control at the vidscreen.

It showed Mok nearing the barge on the river, city lights twinkling in the background.

"But as you can see Mok is alive," Cambridge said. "Very alive."

Beneath the conference table, one of the Committee clutched his hands to his knees in a reaction of panic.

Impossible, this Committee member thought. *I watched Mok die last night. I reported it to the president of the World United. Millions of dollars are about to be wired into my off-shore banking account.*

The Committee member listened to Cambridge as if his life depended on Cambridge's next words. Which it did.

"Why, then, have I called you here if Mok still lives?" Cambridge asked. "Because I know who among you tried to kill him."

CHAPTER 11

CYBERSPACE—PARIS. In the apartment, Mok stood in the dim light of the candle, staring at the spot the dwarf had disappeared from.

It was true, then, that someone was sending him through time. It was true, then, that there was a reason. A direction. And Mok knew now that he was watched, for the dwarf had known of Mok's actions in the other times and places.

But he still had so many questions. What was the reason? What direction? Why was he watched? When would it end?

He knew there was only one way to find out: by going ahead and continuing through life . . . by moving forward, doing the best possible with the knowledge he had . . . and by continuing to learn.

Mok grabbed the sack that held the pieces of the radio. Although not as important as the code book, it was still crucial to remove them from the apartment.

Mok blew out the candle and carefully left the building. Just as carefully—despite Blake's promise of safety—he crept through the alleys of wartime Paris. Within the half hour, he had reached the Seine River.

Paris was well over a thousand years old, and the river had long since been tamed into a wide, slow channel of water. Both sides of the banks were walls built of concrete blocks. The water smelled faintly of damp, moldy cloth. Occasional slaps of water hit the hulls of the boats tied to those walls, and city lights bounced off faint ripples.

It took Mok only a few minutes to find the barge Thaddeus had described. It sat low in the river. There were other flat-bottomed boats as well. They were designed to move cargo slowly down the sluggish river. Each had living quarters on top of the cargo hulls below.

Mok knew from what Thaddeus had said that twenty Jews would later be hidden in the cargo hull, near the bow, behind a false wall. At midnight, French resistance fighters—those secret fighters of the Nazis who occupied Paris—would bring the Jews.

To this point, everything had gone as Thaddeus had promised. Everything had gone, too, as Blake had promised. Except for one thing.

The lights in the windows of the barge.

Mok checked to make sure he'd found the right boat. The dim numbers on the hull were the ones Thaddeus had made him memorize. But there was something wrong.

Thaddeus had made one thing very clear to Mok. The window at the front and the window at the rear would both be lit. Only those two windows. That was the signal that everything was all right. If light shone from any other window, or if either of those two windows was dark, something had gone wrong.

And the rear window was dark.

CHAPTER 12

NOTHING ELSE about the barge seemed unusual. Mok saw no soldiers, no movement. The deck was empty except for coils of rope.

Had Thaddeus forgotten to light the rear window?

Mok wanted to go forward. He wanted to run away. The dwarf's words came back to him. *Does it frighten you to think of the book's power? The lives of thousands upon thousands are in your hands.*

Mok held the small flat notebook tightly against his chest, a reminder of its power. If he went forward and something was wrong, what would happen to the book? If he ran away, could he get the book to those who fought the Nazis?

To do right with the power we have often demands lonely, difficult choices.

Mok decided to go as far as possible—until it appeared danger should turn him back.

He crouched low, moving slowly from shadow to shadow, grateful that his dark clothing helped him to stay hidden. Ten slow minutes later, he was on the deck of the boat, creeping lightly.

Mok reached the front window. He listened. No sounds.

He drew a deep breath and inched his head upward to peek inside. And nearly fell backward.

The light inside clearly showed a small neat cabin with bare walls and a small dining table. Seated at the table were three people. Miriam, Thaddeus, and Wolfgang—the Gestapo officer.

This was not a social event.

Thaddeus and Miriam had their hands tied to the arms of their chairs. Wolfgang, his back to the window, held a pistol in his right hand.

Mok crouched down.

What should he do?

Think, he told himself. *Find a safe place to think*.

Mok crept backward, retracing his steps. He scanned the street, saw no one, and slinked off the barge into deeper shadows.

Hidden, he was deeply conscious of the small notebook. The code book could save thousands upon thousands of lives.

Again, in his mind he heard the dwarf's message.

There is more than one way to get the code book to England.

Indeed, there was. Mok had money. He had survived the street slums of Old Newyork; Paris would be far simpler. Given time, Mok could somehow find a way to get the code book into the right hands.

Yet . . .

He would have to leave Thaddeus and Miriam in the hands of Wolfgang, a Gestapo officer who obviously knew too much about the couple. If Mok ran now, he would condemn his friends to certain punishment, torture, and maybe death. And probably the same fate awaited the twenty Jews who were to arrive at midnight.

Still, the dwarf's words haunted him. *Think of what the book could mean to the world.*

Mok realized the choice was simple. Twenty-two lives against thousands and thousands of lives. Sacrifice only twenty-two and save all those thousands.

But his heart told him differently. Mok could not bring the faces of those thousands into his mind. But all he had to do was close his eyes to see the love that Thaddeus and Miriam had for each other, to see them as they had first embraced on the street, to see Thaddeus comforting Miriam, to see Miriam's fear that a gang might have hurt Thaddeus.

How could Mok let them die?

He now understood what Blake had meant. *To do right with the power we have often demands lonely, difficult choices*. He might be able to ask advice, he might know the rules and laws, he might even face direct commands. But in the end, whatever he chose to do would be a decision he made alone. And how much harder when the choice is not clear . . .

The code book seemed to press heavier and heavier against his chest. Against his heart.

Church bells rang, rolling through the night. Ten bells. Thaddeus had explained to Mok he could measure time by the bells. Two hours left until midnight when the twenty other Jews would arrive. If Mok did nothing, they would be captured.

As Mok waited and agonized in the deep shadows,

he realized something else. He had a third choice: to not make a decision between two choices.

Save thousands and thousands? Or save Thaddeus and Miriam and the others on the barge?

Over and over again, the questions went through his mind.

Mok gritted his teeth.

And finally he decided.

He moved out of the shadows. Without looking back, Mok walked away from the river into the darkness of Paris at night.

CHAPTER 13

MIDNIGHT BELLS rang from a distant church. While the drifting snow had long since stopped falling, bitter cold remained. The sound of the bells seemed as brittle as the air that carried it.

Midnight. When the twenty would gather to be smuggled to safety.

Mok had returned to the river again. This time, however, he did not crouch and move with stealth from shadow to shadow. Instead, he marched boldly onto the barge. He crossed the deck without hesitation, went to the front cabin, and knocked softly.

"Come in," Thaddeus called.

Mok stepped in. He saw only Thaddeus and Miriam. Until Wolfgang, hidden behind the open door, calmly shut it.

"Finally," Wolfgang said, pistol at Mok's face. "Our little pigeon arrives."

Mok let his mouth drop.

"Come, come," Wolfgang said. "Must you be so surprised? We Gestapo are far ahead of the pitiful resistance movement."

"Thaddeus?" Mok said.

"I am terribly sorry," Thaddeus said. "We were—"

"Fools," Wolfgang broke in. "Thinking I had

actually let them go. You see, informers told us of their plan to escape with twenty other Jews. I arranged for them to be thrown out of their apartment. I arranged to be there to offer them help. But, of course, it was a trap."

"A second car was following behind," Thaddeus said, miserable. "It was the one that nearly hit you. When Wolfgang drove away, spies in the other car jumped out down the street and came back to follow us. When they realized Le Café Bordeaux was not our meeting place, they simply captured us again."

"I put a gun to his head," Wolfgang said. "But this stubborn old man was willing to die before telling me where he intended to meet the others. So I told him he could watch his wife die slowly instead." Wolfgang smiled with evil. "Then he told me everything."

The Gestapo officer glanced at his watch. "I expect the other Jews to arrive within minutes. There are soldiers below in the cargo hold waiting to capture them and send them to work camps. Since you have helped these Jews, you must suffer with them."

Mok showed fear. "No!" he cried. "I have something you want. Let me trade that for my life!"

"What could you have that I might want?" Wolfgang asked with a sneer.

Mok pulled a piece of paper from his pocket. He unfolded it and handed it to the officer.

"What is this?" Wolfgang asked, glancing at the scribbled notes.

"One page from a notebook that belongs to Thaddeus."

"No!" Thaddeus shouted. "You cannot tell him about the code book!"

"For my life I can," Mok said. Mok turned to Wolfgang and continued to speak. "You'll see that Thaddeus has unlocked a radio code. The top half shows the radio message. The bottom half shows what the code means."

Wolfgang stared hard at Mok.

"Sit against the wall," Wolfgang finally ordered. "I want to read this without wondering when you will jump at me."

Mok sat.

A half minute later, Wolfgang spoke again. "This is indeed important. Tell me more."

Mok did. Mok told Wolfgang about the crystal radio. About Thaddeus and his background. And about how Thaddeus had sent Mok back to the apartment for the code book.

When Mok finished, Wolfgang stroked his mustache. "Why shouldn't I just kill you now and search your body for the code book?"

Mok reached inside his jacket and pulled out a small black notebook. He tossed it to Wolfgang. "Because the one I carry is a fake. The other one is hidden. I intended to go to England with the Jews and, once safely there, sell the location of the real one for a fortune."

"Which you will now give to me instead?" Wolfgang asked, smirking.

"All I want is my life," Mok said.

"You cannot make that trade!" Thaddeus shouted. "It is worth our own lives to stop the invasion of England!"

"Shut up, old man," Mok said. "You are much nearer the grave than I. Life is still precious to me."

Thaddeus gaped at Mok. "You vile traitor. At least the Nazis make no disguise of their hatred. You pose as a friend and turn on us. May your soul rot forever. May—"

To stop Thaddeus's rising rage, Wolfgang lifted his hand to strike Miriam.

"Enough," Wolfgang said. "I want the code book. Where is it?"

Mok smiled. "Hidden on the barge, so I would have it near once we made it to England. Yes, I know you could easily kill me once you find it. But I believe this proves I can be of service to you in the future."

Wolfgang smiled back. "That is more than a possibility. You do appear to be a capable young man. Tell me where it is."

"No farther than the inside of a life jacket on the far side of the deck." Mok made motions as if to rise. "Shall I get it for you?"

"Am I stupid enough to let you go alone?" Wolfgang said. "Hardly. We'll go together. And quickly, before the other Jews arrive to be captured."

Mok stood.

"Hands on your head," Wolfgang said. "I will follow you."

Mok opened the door slowly and then obediently placed his hands on top of his head. The cold night air hit him hard. He took a deep breath and stepped forward, knowing the outcome of the war depended on the next few seconds.

CHAPTER 14

MOK MOVED SLOWLY. He did not want Wolfgang walking quickly.

One step. Two. Mok waited . . .

Then it happened. The loud thump. A muffled yell. The two resistance fighters on the roof had tackled Wolfgang!

Mok began to turn in triumph. But a loud roar and a bright burst knocked him to the deck.

Mok fell, twisted, one leg bent beneath the other.

For several shocked seconds, he didn't move. He stared up at the glow of lights from the city bouncing off low clouds.

He struggled to figure out what had made the noise and the bright burst. He tried to sit up.

He could do neither.

Pain hit. A surge of white heat flamed from his chest and spread through his body.

Still, Mok did not understand.

"He's been shot!" Mok heard a voice say. But the voice seemed distant, as if coming from the far end of a tunnel. "Get a cloth to stop the bleeding."

Shot?

A face bent over him.

"Can you hear me?" the man asked. It was one

of the resistance fighters. A small compact man. Mok knew his name. Pierre. They'd spoken less than a half hour earlier. "Can you hear me?"

What a dumb question, Mok thought. He said so to Pierre. In Mok's mind, he was talking clearly. But for some reason, Pierre didn't seem to understand.

Another man crouched down beside Pierre. Thaddeus.

"He's in shock," Pierre said to the old man. "I don't know what we can do to bring him back."

What did Pierre mean, bring him back? Where was he going? Mok tried to disagree, but he couldn't make his lips speak.

Darkness began to close in. Not the sudden whirling darkness that had sent him to the Holy Land from ancient Egypt.

This was a different darkness. A cold darkness where silence seemed to echo.

Sadness filled Mok. How could he now explain everything to Thaddeus? How he'd gone to retrieve the radio pieces because he knew Thaddeus would need it to find another way to escape. How he'd waited near the barge for the resistance fighters to appear with the Jews. How he'd told them of his plan to fool Wolfgang into stepping outside. How he'd actually thrown Wolfgang the real code book, hoping he could bluff Wolfgang. How . . .

Dimly, Mok saw that Miriam was on her knees, holding his hand and Thaddeus was bent in prayer.

And dimly . . .

The blackness and silence became complete.

CHAPTER 15

MAINSIDE. Cambridge paced before the Committee. "Each of you, I'm sure, remembers the day we discovered a killer had been cybered onto the pirate ship."

Nods came from around the table.

"You will remember how our comtechs took so long to cyber Mok to the next site."

More nods.

Cambridge continued. "That night, I called each of you privately. I asked you to be the secondary backup of the password code that allowed access to the cybersite."

Again, more nods, this time with puzzled faces. Behind Cambridge, the three-dimensional images of Mok in cyberspace flickered silently across the vidscreen. But all eyes were on Cambridge.

Especially the eyes of one man. A man whose throat was dry with fear.

"Well," Cambridge said, "I gave a different password code to each Committee member. Ones that would put you each into a different ghost-site."

"Ghost-site?" one of the Committee asked.

"Ghost-site," Cambridge said. "A site that mirrored Mok's actual cybersite. But was not hooked to

Mok's virtual reality. We had twelve ghost-sites. That's what took the comtechs so long—getting those sites ready."

"I don't understand," another member said. "Why go to all the trouble?"

"Then all we needed to do was monitor the ghost-sites," Cambridge answered. "Since each of you was given a password to a different site, when the cyberassassin appeared on a specific ghost-site, we would have our traitor. And last night, we discovered who it was."

Cambridge closed his eyes briefly, as if dreading the announcement.

Before he could speak, someone pointed at the screen and shouted.

"Mok! He's been shot!"

CHAPTER 16

CYBERSPACE—JERUSALEM. SHOUTS. WAILING. BABBLE.
Dust. Heat. Sun. Shadows.

Slowly, one by one, Mok made sense of each new impression. It seemed an icy blackness was melting away from him, bringing him into growing light.

Mok became aware of hard stone pressing against his body, of rough walls around him. He smelled vegetables and fruit left to rot. He took in the shapes of the archways and the tiled roofs. It reminded him somewhat of the streets he'd seen in Egypt, except this seemed more crowded.

The noise and babble grew louder as he walked toward the street. Why was he in pain as he walked? A man heard Mok gasp with agony and turned toward him.

"My friend," the man said, "you are in a bad way."

The man was black haired and bearded, with a square face and dark eyes. Despite his bulk, he did not appear intimidating.

"Where . . ." Mok gasped at the effort it took to speak. "Where are we?"

The man frowned. "Jerusalem. During Passover. Did the thieves beat you so badly that you cannot remember?"

"It hurts," Mok said. He could not remember ever in his lifetime in the slums asking for help. Weakness meant death in Old Newyork. But Mok had little more strength than a newborn baby. And there was something gentle about this large man.

"Please help me . . ."

AUTHOR NOTE

Mok's story is actually two stories. One of the stories is described in this cyberepisode.

There is also a series story linking together all the CyberQuest books—the reason Mok has been sent into cyberspace. That story starts in Pharaoh's Tomb *(#1) and is completed in* Galilee Man *(#6). No matter where you start reading Mok's story, you can easily go back to the beginning of the series without feeling like you already know too much about how the series story will end.*

This series story takes place about a hundred years in the future. You will see that parts of Mok's world are dark and grim. Yet, in the end, this is a story of hope, the most important hope any of us can have. We, too, live in a world that at times can be dark and grim. During his cyberquest, Mok will see how Jesus Christ and his followers have made a difference over the ages.

Some of you may be reading these books after following Mok's adventures in Breakaway, *a Focus on the Family magazine for teen guys. Those magazine episodes were the inspiration for the* CyberQuest *series, and I would like to thank Michael Ross and Jesse Flores at* Breakaway *for* all the fun we had working together. However, this series contains far more than the original stories—once I really started to explore Mok's world, it became obvious to me that there was too much of the story left to be told. So, if you're joining this adventure because of Breakaway, I think I can still promise you plenty of surprises.

Last, thank you for sharing Mok's world with me. You are the ones who truly bring Mok and his friends and enemies to life.

From your friend,

Sigmund Brouwer

The adventure continues!

Join Mok for
the conclusion of CyberQuest in

QUEST 6

GALILEE MAN

From century to century, Mok has been
searching for the Galilee Man. In ancient
Jerusalem, where people screamed commands
to crucify a simple carpenter, Mok's quest may
finally end. Yet if he survives, there remains
the danger facing him in Old Newyork,
two thousand years into the future . . .